Dedicated to:

All the neurodiverse people who

have yet to find their voice, place,

or space

Introduction

Being neurodiverse can be hard. Really hard. Having a condition that makes you experience the world in different ways than others can sometimes make you feel excluded, or even downright bullied. And society doesn't help. Those who identify as neurotypical (normal) usually write off neurodiverse people as being "weird," or "off," and thus create societal systems not well-designed for people who think, see, and feel the world around them differently.

One of the most prominent examples of this is in our education system, where students who don't perform "normally" are often given inadequate support and harsh discipline. In this book, you can put yourself into the shoes of a neurodiverse high school student as you try to navigate the trials and tribulations of an unforgiving environment - and, conversely, the success you experience when given the opportunity to flourish.

This book was written using OpenDyslexic, a font specifically designed to maximize ease of readability for people with dyslexia. Read more at opendyslexic.com.

About the Conditions

In this book, you are put into the shoes of a neurodiverse high school student with Autism and ADHD.

Autism is a condition characterized by a different outlook and approach to social interactions. Autistic people are also noted for their ability to hyper-focus, or concentrate keenly on a task for hours on end, if they enjoy the topic they're working on.

ADHD is a condition that makes it difficult to concentrate for long periods of time, often caused by a difficulty to control impulses. On the other hand, people with ADHD are often very creatively-minded and highly energetic.

Throughout the book, you will see portions of the story that are highlighted and footnoted. These passages correspond to an explanation of a corresponding symptom or strength of one of the conditions (ADHD, Autism) and is explained at the end of the book.

In Their Shoes

August 20th. A blisteringly hot, humid day somewhere in suburbia. As you pull up to the curb, your new high school appears.

Boy, am I excited, you think.

First day of school! What can go wrong?

As you open the doors, you enter a new world. A zoo of sights, smells, and sounds confronts you like a wall.

High school sure is different.

Overwhelmed physically and emotionally, you do your best to remain composed. You focus on each and every detail in the scene unfolding in front of you[6]. The bell rings. A sea of students flood like a tidal wave through the locker-adorned faux-granite corridors, jockeying for position.

Why can't people just...walk normally?

Suddenly, the sea of students parts. Nerds, jocks, and everything in between hug the walls as they stampede to class. They know to always give the bully his space as he swaggers down the hallways with an ego too big for even this stately high school. This is his turf. But swamped with sensory overload, you don't know how to react - and head right into the lion's den. A hulking, pock-marked student awaits you as you run straight into his chest. A ring of his sidekicks flank your left and right.

"Now what do we have here?" the bully asks his allies.

The whole school comes to a standstill. Your hall has become a coliseum, and you're the main attraction.

"Well, you gonna say something or what?"

DO YOU:
Stand Up for Yourself?
Continue Reading.

Stay Quiet?
Turn to Page 5.

2

You have trouble understanding social situations[1]. Overwhelmed with emotion and unable to control your anger, you blurt out the first words that come to mind.

"Yeah, I'm gonna say something. Leave me alone."

As you look around the crowd, time comes to a standstill. A group of kids in the crowd let out barely audible gasps. Others open their mouths wide in disbelief.

"You think our little buddy is asking for something?" the bully asks sarcastically.

"Well, if they insist, I guess I must deliver."

The next thing you know, you awaken, lying down on an uncomfortable blue medical bed.

"Am I...dead?"

A harsh, grating voice greets you from behind.

"Nah, you're just in the nurse's office. You came pretty close to it though. My goodness, you got rocked."

"W-w-well...if I'm ok now, can I go back to cla-?"

The nurse interrupts you.

"First, I'm gonna have to run some tests on you."

"Oh, okay."

The nurse asks you to go through various exercises to make sure you're physically okay. You have a hard time completing the tasks she asks of you, and you end up failing the tests. You also have a hard time vocalizing your conditions to the nurse.

"Well, I can't say much about what I'm seeing. I mean, if you WANT to go to class, I won't stop you. But since it's only your first day, you can go home if you want. The choice is yours."

For you, going about your daily routine can be quite hard[2]. This morning, you had a hard time getting your lunch together, and you ended up bringing just an apple. Eventually, however, you make a choice.

DO YOU:
Go to Class?
Turn to Page 10.

Go Home?
Turn to Page 9.

You feel a rush of adrenaline as your mind races with tons of witty remarks. But since you want to keep your body in one piece, you decide to say nothing. You try your best to sink back into the crowded hallway and make your way to class.

"Why would you do that? Do you not know how to be a normal kid?" a student asks you.

What a great first impression. You shake your head and keep walking.

The hall seems to stretch on forever. You keep replaying the bully's actions back in your head as you hurriedly walk down the corridor[3].

If only I knew how to keep my head down and follow the pack. If only I knew how to be normal.

What you wouldn't realize is that society, not you, is at fault. You keep walking. What seems like 20 steps for others feels like a thousand for you. For you, even the most mundane actions require lots of attention.

As you approach the classroom door, a wave of anger, regret, and resentment bubbles to the surface. You have a hard time holding these emotions in. But your conditions make you feel the need to let them out.

DO YOU:
Express your feelings?
Continue Reading.

Sweep it under the rug?
Turn to Page 10.

You can't help it. You let out a scream. You stomp on the ground with enough force to cause an earthquake. You let your anger, exasperation, and fear all out. After all, you experience high-stress scenarios, like crowds, much differently than most people[6].

All of a sudden, everything is calm. Too calm. You notice that everyone has stopped what they were doing. You look up, no longer absorbed in your own (rightful) feelings. Then, you notice it.

Everyone's looking at you.

The stares.

As you continue to walk down the hall to your classroom. You try to keep your head down. But you can still *feel* the stares. Each one pierces you like a spear.

What did I do wrong? you ask yourself.

You were only trying to express your feelings, like everyone else. You know you need to go to class, but you figure nobody could blame you for wanting to sit it out for a bit, especially after what you've just been through. A dilemma is on your hands.

DO YOU:
Go to Class?
Turn to *Page 10.*

Take a Breather?
Turn to *Page 12.*

You're given a pass to go home. After all, you have been through a lot, since you experience emotional drainage much faster than others[6]. So, you head back down the long, imposing hallway from whence you came. You pass the spot that, just a few minutes ago, was a boxing ring with you as a fighter.

Why couldn't I have kept my mouth shut?

As you leave the building and exit into the plaza outside, the sunlight hits you like a freight train. Yet, even still, you remain persistent in thinking about the day's events[3].

Why couldn't I have kept my mouth shut?

As you continue on your walk home, the regret you feel for your actions (which you couldn't help at the time) pounds at your head like a mallet on a drum. The mallet beats faster. You ignore the passers-by who see your cuts and bruises and ask if you're ok[3].

Once you arrive home, you look for something to take your mind off of today's events. Because of sensory needs from your Autism, you think doing some chores or drawing might be a good distraction.

DO YOU:
Draw?
Turn to *Page 14.*

Do Chores?
Turn to *Page 16.*

Finally, you think.

After all that, I can finally go to class.

The bell rings. You find an open desk towards the front of the classroom.

"Alright, students. Welcome to class," the teacher says.

Oh, no. Your worst nightmare. A class you're not interested in. You're able to focus very deeply on subjects you like — but you hate this subject, so you have a hard time paying attention[7]. Just 30 minutes into the lecture, your attention starts to wane. You try to resist the urge to talk to a nearby classmate, but you eventually give in.

You slyly whip out your phone and try to text with someone you knew from middle school. You have a hard time understanding the tone that your classmate is speaking in, so you eventually stop texting out of exasperation[1].

"This class is so stupid," you whisper.

Or, at least you think you whispered. It's hard for you to control your impulses or pick up on social cues, which meant that you ended up saying that a *little* too loud[1].

Everyone appears to have heard you, and it's déjà vu all over again as dozens of eyeballs rest their gazes on you.

"Is there anything else you have to say?" your teacher angrily asks you.

"N-no, sorry. Carry on."

Class continues without a hitch. That is, until you hear your teacher say all of the material mentioned today will be on the midterm. And the final.

Aw, crap. I have to talk to my teacher about getting accommodations.

After school, you walk up to him and mention the accommodations you need, petrified by what his response might be. You know how this conversation went in middle school, and you're not optimistic.

"We don't do that here," your teacher remarks. "Especially after how you disrespected my class. Now get out of my room; class is over and I gotta head home."

Wow. First day of class and it's this bad already. Luckily for you, class is out for the day and you only have a few hours before you can head home. But you hardly know anyone at your new school, so that means either making new friends or sitting alone with a book your mom packed you.

DO YOU:
Try to Hang Out?
Turn to Page 17.

Read a Book?
Turn to Page 19.

11

Good move, you think to yourself. You needed a break anyway. Especially since you hate the class you're missing.

For a solid 10 minutes, you're hunched over your phone at the base of the lockers in the hall. You're emotionally drained from all the sensory exposure you've experienced so far[6]. Each crowd, bully, or stare you've gotten has taken something out of your energy. And you need to recharge.

All seems well until an imposing figure approaches you. He looks angry, although you have a hard time figuring out exactly what he's feeling[1].

"And what do you think you're doing?" the man asks with a stern expression.

God, did the bully grow taller or something? you think.

After an awkward pause, the man continues, "I'm the principal. And I'm here to ask why you're sitting in the middle of the hall during class. Care to explain?"

You're mortified. Ever since you were young, you didn't know how to behave anytime an unfamiliar authority figure gets angry. You try to find the words to explain yourself, but they're just not there[5]. And even worse, you start thinking about other, more interesting stuff as the principal starts lecturing you[7]. But you do manage to catch one important piece of information before he finishes.

"...and that's it! I will not tolerate disrespect like this in my high school. You are going to have to leave. And there will be additional discipline."

Turn Back to Page 9.

13

Safe from an oppressive school environment, you take the opportunity to decompress. Having settled into your couch, an enormous weight feels as if it has been lifted from your shoulders.

I should go draw, you think to yourself.

Reluctantly, you arise from your comfy leather couch, look for your colored pens, and get to work. Because one of your greatest strengths is the ability to persevere in activities you love, you work nonstop[3][4] on your sketchpad. And, as you lose track of time easily[2], you put your mind to it for hours.

"Come down for dinner!" your mom yells up the stairs.

"Can't, give me 5!"

Unbeknownst to your laser-focused mind, an hour passes.

"Help me with the dishes!"

"One sec!"

Yet another unsuspecting hour passes. You continue drawing.

"Honey, it's 10 o'clock at night. You have school tomorrow! Get to bed."

"No, it's 7:30."

A quick glance at your alarm clock confirms that your mom was right. But your work wasn't for nothing. Your once-bare sketchpad is now brimming end-to-end with beautiful artwork. In a place that valued you for your strengths instead of picking on your challenges, you thrived. And now, it's time for you to get some sleep and get ready for another day of school to come.

THE END

15

You're finally home. Away from the outright emotional damage your school has caused you, you can finally rest. And nothing does that job better than a few chores.

"Mom, I'm home! Anything you need?"

"Yeah, honey, how about a break? Why don't you go do some dishes or something?"

You heed her advice and plow through 5 and a half loads of dishes. By the time you pull your hands from the sink, your fingers are so pruned from the water that their tips look like raisins. But you don't notice that.

"My goodness, you've been working for hours! It's almost dinner!"

"W-what do you mean? I just got home 10 minutes ago!"

Because of your autism, you're able to devote great attention to things you enjoy doing; however, you also aren't the greatest at keeping time[2]. As it turns out, you've been doing dishes for over 4 hours.

"Come, take a seat. Go unwind. You know you have another busy day tomorrow!"

You heed her advice. Exhausted, mentally and physically from your day, you can't wait to kick back on the old leather couch and play some video games. The floral aroma of pot roast fills the air as dinner draws near. And as you settle in, you think of the trials and tribulations that await you in the days, weeks, and months to come.

THE END

Oh god. Social connections. My favorite.

You try to approach a stranger in the social jungle outside the school entrance. What others don't understand is that you don't know any of the rules governing this jungle that came naturally to those around you[1]. As you search for someone to talk to, the massive gothic facade of the main building glares at you, disapprovingly.

You walk around the lawn, desperate for someone to offer you a social lifeline. But your classmates didn't forget what had happened that morning. They want nothing to do with you.

"Why can't I just be normal?" you mutter quietly to yourself.

Then, a response.

"You are normal. Just like me."

Startled, you swivel your head around to find the source of the noise. You see a student with gigantic glasses who stands about a foot away, smiling.

"Lemme guess. You're different too?" the kid asks.

"How could you tell?" you reply back, with a little more sarcasm than you intended.

"Well, I've got Autism, Dysphonia, and Light Sensitivity. So call it a sixth sense. Nice to meet you!"

"You too," you manage to say back, despite being a little startled at your new friend's in-your-face introduction.

"You know, I don't have any work I need to do tonight — wanna come hang out?"

Before you get a chance to think about it, your vocal cords do the thinking for you.

"Sure, I'd love to."

On the long trek back to your new friend's place, you question why you feel so much happier now compared to just a few hours ago. Upon further contemplation, you find the answer: you're in an environment that supports you. And as you lie on the couch with your newly-made pal playing video games, thinking of just how far you can go with the right support, you realize that you – and the conditions that made you, you – were never abnormal. Society was.

THE END

You rifle through your overstuffed backpack in search of a book.

I better not have left it at home, you think.

As the summer heat blasts at you without rest, you continue scrounging around in your bag until you feel the glossy corner of a paperback.

A Neurodiverse Kid's Guide to Making Their Own Inclusive Environment, the title reads.

Your eyes then dart to the corner of the book, where your mom left a taped sticky note reading *see this if you're ever in trouble :)* Interested, you do as the note commands.

Page 27. *How to navigate situations with a bully.*

Boy, I could have used this.

Page 48. Educating *teachers on alternative methods to teach people like you.*

I really should have read that sticky note in the morning.

As you read on, your head fills with different ways to change your school for the better. One of your greatest strengths, as a person with Autism, is the ability to think differently than others. Reflecting on all you've gone through, you can also thank your ADHD for making you so resilient and creative. Throughout the rest of the day, you use these strengths to dream up limitless ways to help educate others of the struggles you and others similar to you face every day. Once society learns that their treatment of people like you, rather than you yourself, is the real abnormality, maybe they'll start to change.

THE END

Footnotes + Explanations

1. **Difficulty with Social Cues**: Both people with ADHD and Autism have a common difficulty of picking up social cues. People with ADHD have a hard time sharing/taking turns in a conversation or check-out of a conversation where they are bored. Autistic people often have trouble picking up social cues that are not direct, such as changes in tone, gestures, or even sarcastic remarks.

2. **Executive Dysfunction**: Executive function skills enable us to plan, focus attention, remember instructions, and manage multiple tasks. Individuals with executive dysfunction struggle with planning, problem-solving, organization, and time management. Autistic people often struggle with maintaining good executive function skills.

3. **Hyperfocus**: Hyperfocus is a phenomenon that reflects one's complete absorption in a task, to a point where a person appears to completely ignore or 'tune out' everything else. It is generally reported to occur when a person is engaged in an activity that is particularly fun or interesting.

4. **Special Interests**: Special interests are frequently developed by individuals with autism spectrum disorder, expressed as an intense focus on specific topics. Neurotypical individuals also develop special interests, often in the form of hobbies.

Footnotes, Continued

5. **Autistic Meltdowns/Shutdowns**: An Autistic meltdown is an intense response to an overwhelming situation. It happens when someone becomes completely overwhelmed by their current situation and temporarily loses control of their behavior. This loss of control can be expressed verbally, physically, or in both ways.

6. **Sensory Overload**: Autistic people are often more prone to sensory overload, where they get more input from their senses than their brain can process. This can lead to stress, irritability, and restlessness around heavy sensory stimuli such as loud noises, bright lights, as well as certain fabrics.

7. **Trouble Paying Attention**: Both people who have Autism and ADHD may have difficulty paying attention. In particular, Autistic people may have difficulty with activities that involve shared attention, like reading a book with a carer, doing a puzzle, or even walking safely across the road. People with ADHD may have difficulty paying attention due to distractions, lack of interest, or issues with hyperactivity.

[Note: The experiences listed above are a few common examples of things people with Autism and ADHD face. This list is not intended to be entirely representative of the whole broader, more nuanced experiences faced by these individuals.]

Acknowledgements

Thank you so much to our wonderful mentors: Esperanza Padilla, Isabelle Hsu, Dr. Lawrence Fung, and the countless others at SNP-REACH 2022 who helped us find our voice. We couldn't have made this book without your help! Also, a huge thanks goes out to the folks at Stanford's Neurodiversity Special Interest Group, who graciously provided feedback on improving our early drafts.

SNP REACH 2022

Our Mentors!

Esperanza Padilla is a mentor on this project. She is a Neurodiverse researcher who discovered her Autism/ADHD later in life. She is currently a graduate student at UCSF's Ph.D. program for the Sociology of Medicine and looks forward to connecting research and advocacy.

Isabelle Hsu is a mentor on this project. She is a neurodiverse high school senior who was diagnosed early in elementary school. She attended Stanford Neurodiversity Project (SNP) REACH summer camp in 2020 and started advocacy work at her high school and community, as well as research in the field. She currently serves as co-chair of SNP's Network for K-12 Neurodiversity Education and Advocacy (NNEA) and is exploring various possibilities of combining her strengths with her passion in neurodiversity advocacy.

About the Authors

Gavin Griffin is the lead writer and head coordinator of this project. He is a rising junior at Bellarmine College Preparatory in San Jose, California. A nationally-recognized speech-and-debater, Gavin enjoys using his voice to uplift and empower neurodiverse students. In his free time, you can find Gavin playing basketball (badly) with his friends, practicing his favorite Chopin etude, or taking care of his pet chickens. Using the knowledge he gained from SNP-REACH, Gavin hopes to research and implement thoughtful solutions to pressing problems in society at the intersection of medicine, sociology, business, and engineering.

Rui (Rose) Kong is a lead illustrator on this project. She is a senior at Los Alamitos High School in southern California. In her free time, she enjoys drawing and playing badminton. She has been drawing for more than 13 years. In the future, she is going to apply the knowledge learned from SNP-REACH 2022 to her own Neurodiversity club and research projects.

Tanvi Vidyala is a lead illustrator on this project. She is neurodiverse and a senior at American High School in Northern California. Inspired by the experiences of herself and others she wanted to find ways to best promote self-advocacy in the neurodiverse community. She hopes to study psychology, linguistics, education, and design. She is a member of her school's theatre productions and a classically trained vocalist. In her free time she enjoys making music, reading, and games on her Nintendo Switch.

Cate Marshburn is an illustrator on this project. She is a high school Junior from Texas who grew a passion to learn more about neurodiversity and advocacy through her experiences with her Autistic family member. She participates heavily at her school, from band to book clubs, and hopes to be able to use her new knowledge and experiences to better advocate for neurodiverse individuals in her community.

Taj Jawanda is a writer and editor on this project. He is a rising senior at Amador Valley High School in Pleasanton, California. In his free time, he enjoys biking with his friends, playing sports such as football and basketball, as well as listening to music while dialing in intense tasks. His future goals relate to using the knowledge he has accumulated from SNP-REACH to implement ways of fostering inclusivity in the environment around him. Going into college, he will pursue the pre-med route as his ambition lies in attending medical school in the hopes of becoming a doctor.

Rayna Vora is a writer and editor on this project. She is a senior at Foothill High School in California. In her free time, she enjoys swimming, playing the piano, reading classics, and listening to many genres of music. She hopes to take her experiences from SNP-REACH 2022 and implement them at schools all over the globe. In the future, she wants to further her involvement in neurodiversity advocacy through fostering representation & inclusivity. She would like to pursue an education in psychology in college.

Kevin Rha is a writer and editor on this project. He is a senior at Montgomery Blair High School in Maryland. He loves to run and play the violin, and in his free time listens to music and podcasts. Having accumulated leadership experience with the many clubs he is involved in he hopes to continue advocating for neurodiversity at not only his high school but continually. He would like to study applied mathematics and neuroscience in college.

Printed in the USA
CPSIA information can be obtained
at www.ICGtesting.com
LVHW062143180124
769375LV00038B/229